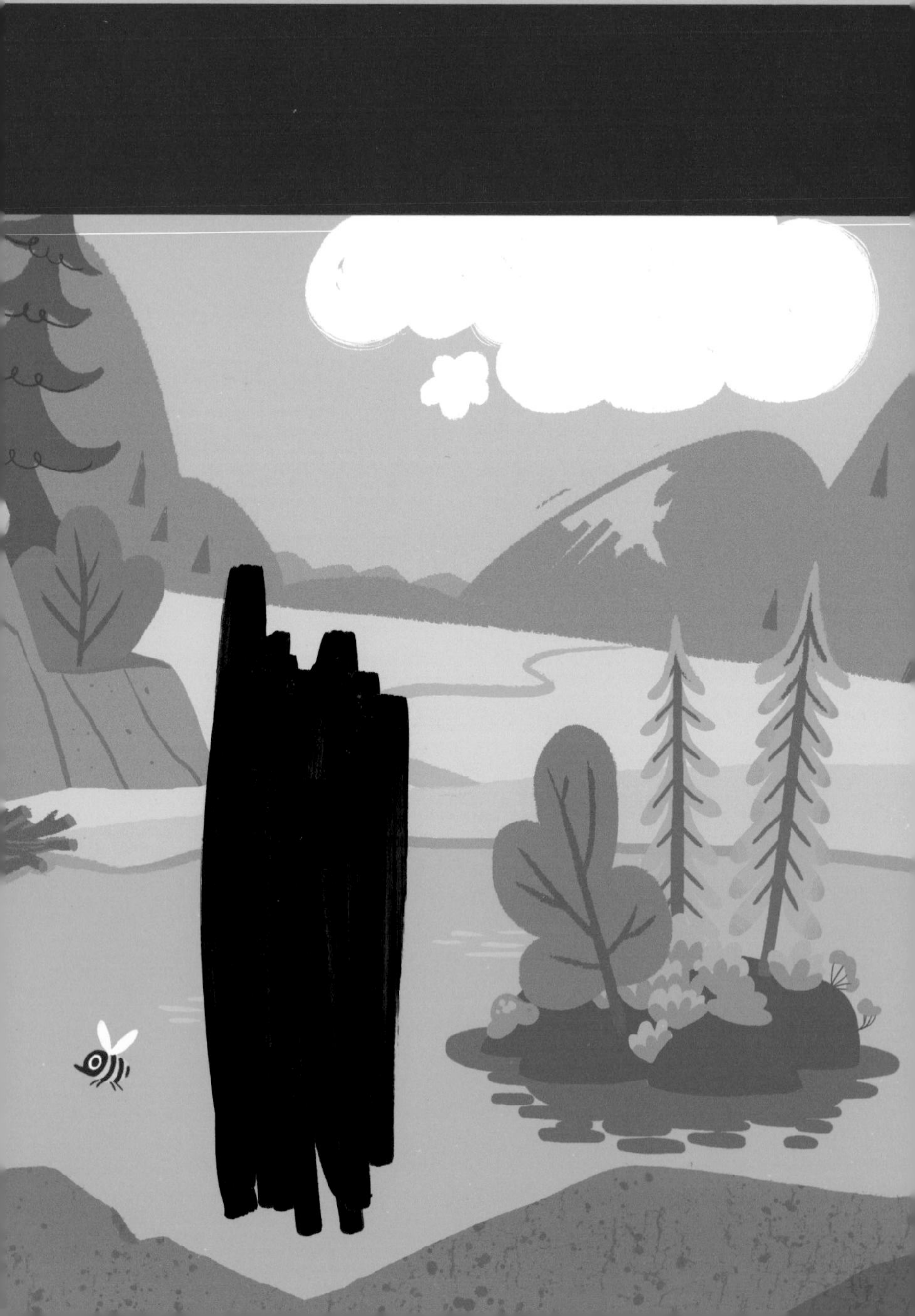

# COOL SCHOOL

# DREW PENDOUS

## and the
## *Camp Color War*

*adapted by*
**David Lewman**
*based on the screenplay by*
**Rachel O. Crouse**

*illustrated by*
**Robert Zress**
*art direction by*
**Dan Markowitz**

*based on the series*
**COOL SCHOOL**
*and characters*
*created by*
**Rob Kurtz**

STERLING CHILDREN'S BOOKS
New York

**STERLING CHILDREN'S BOOKS**
New York

An Imprint of Sterling Publishing Co., Inc.
1166 Avenue of the Americas
New York, NY 10036

ISBN 978-1-4549-3107-2

Distributed in Canada by Sterling Publishing Co., Inc.
c/o Canadian Manda Group, 664 Annette Street
Toronto, Ontario M6S 2C8, Canada
Distributed in the United Kingdom by GMC Distribution Services
Castle Place, 166 High Street, Lewes, East Sussex BN7 1XU, England
Distributed in Australia by NewSouth Books
University of New South Wales, Sydney, NSW 2052, Australia

For information about custom editions, special sales, and premium and corporate purchases, please contact Sterling Special Sales at 800-805-5489 or specialsales@sterlingpublishing.com.

Manufactured in China

Lot #:
2 4 6 8 10 9 7 5 3
06/19

sterlingpublishing.com

# CONTENTS

## CHAPTER ONE

**YES,** it's time for another **amazing adventure** starring everyone's favorite superhero . . .

THE STUPENDOUS

# DREW PENDOUS

AND HIS MIGHTY PEN ULTIMATE!

Ah, good ol' summertime! When Drew and all his friends from Cool School went to . . .

CAMP COOL SCHOOL!

the coolest summer camp EVER!!!

"I **love** Camp Cool School," Drew said happily. "It's the coolest!"

Camp Cool School was up in the mountains next to a clear, blue lake. All around the camp were shady woods.

"There are a **_ton_** of fun things to do at Camp Cool School," Drew said.

He was right.

You could
**_swim_**
in the lake.

You could **_sing songs_** around a campfire.

You could go for a **_hike_**.

You could **paddle a canoe** or a kayak.

You could play **baseball** or **soccer**.

"And don't forget the crafts!" Crafty Carol said. "At Camp Cool School, we make lots of **cool, woodsy crafts.**"

At Camp Cool School, Drew's teachers were the camp counselors. Let's see. . . . Who else was at Camp Cool School that summer?

MS. BOOKSY!

LET'S READ SPOOKY STORIES BY THE CAMPFIRE.

CRAFTY CAROL!

THEY ALREADY KNOW I'M HERE. REMEMBER?

OH, YEAH!

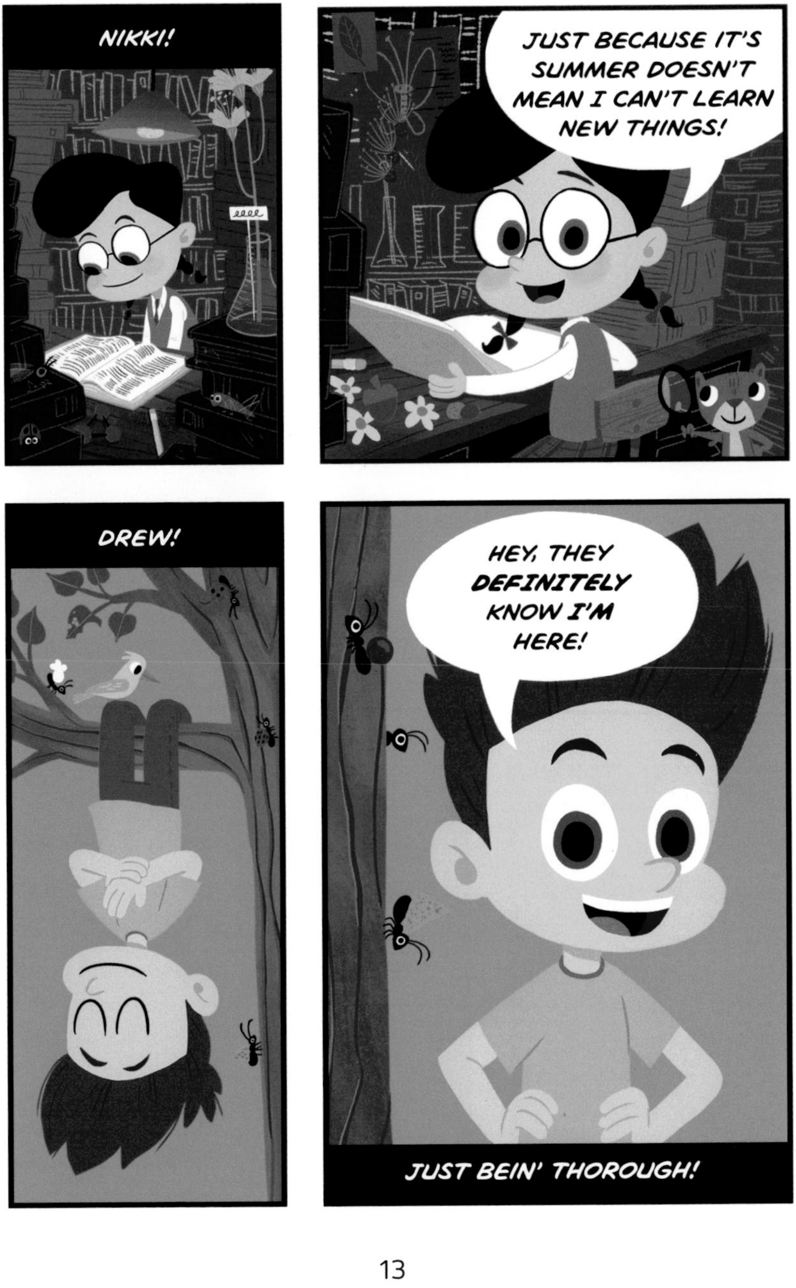
NIKKI!
JUST BECAUSE IT'S SUMMER DOESN'T MEAN I CAN'T LEARN NEW THINGS!
DREW!
HEY, THEY DEFINITELY KNOW I'M HERE!
JUST BEIN' THOROUGH!

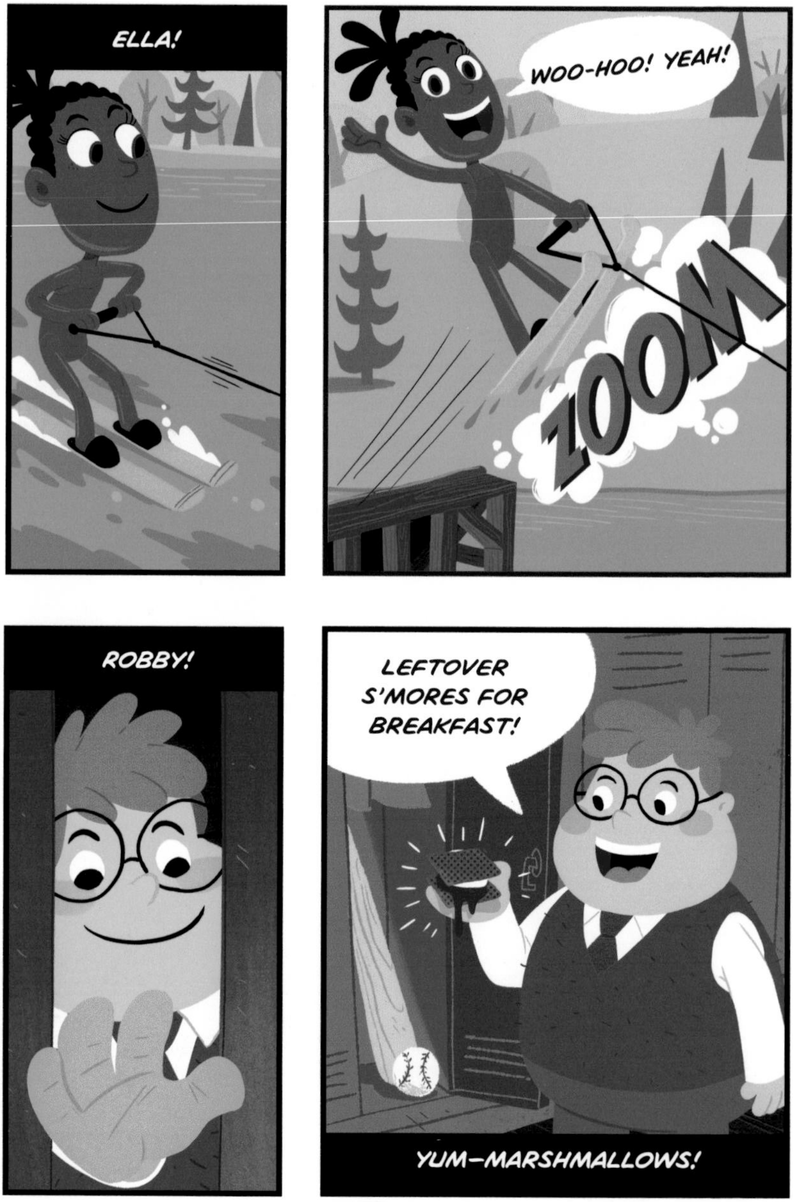
ELLA!
WOO-HOO! YEAH!
ZOOM
ROBBY!
LEFTOVER S'MORES FOR BREAKFAST!
YUM—MARSHMALLOWS!

AND . . . SIMON THE FROG?

OH, I'VE GOT AN IMPORTANT PART TO PLAY. . . . YOU'LL SEE!

ALL AT . . . **CAMP COOL SCHOOL!**

Drew was superexcited. On the last day of Camp Cool School, all the campers wore blue. They were ready for . . .

the COLOR WAR!

A color war was when one team wore one color (like blue) and competed against a team of rival campers from across the lake that wore a different color (like red). There were lots of contests, and whichever team had the most points at the end of the day won the color war.

Dressed in blue, the Camp Cool School team members met on the morning of the color war. Drew used his Pen Ultimate, which magically brought everything he drew to life,  to dress himself in his blue superhero costume.

"Okay, Team Blue!" Drew said. "We've never met these campers, so we don't know how big they are."

"Or how crafty," added Crafty Carol.

"Or how smart," Nikki chimed in.

But Drew wasn't worried about the other team. Not one bit. "I KNOW we can win," he said confidently. "Team Red's got nothing on us!"

Everybody cheered.

"Wait," Nikki said, looking around. "Where IS Team Red?"

"Here we are," said a familiar raspy voice. "Ready to play?"

They all turned to see who had spoken.

Ray Blank was Drew's evil twin. This meant that the camp across the lake had to be **CAMP CRUEL SCHOOL!**

## CHAPTER TWO

**CRUEL SCHOOL** was full of villains and bad guys who were learning how to be mean, nasty, and rude. That is, **even** meaner, nastier, and ruder.

The evildoers took classes in teasing, mocking, bullying, stealing, and scheming.

They had homework assignments like "Describe ten ways to ruin someone's day. Then **go ruin someone's day**."

At the end of every year, Cruel School gave out awards like Least Courteous,

Most Improved in Awfulness, Most Likely to Cause a Disaster, and Greatest Grump.

In the summer, the students at Cruel School packed up their tricks, pranks, and plans to take over the world and headed to Camp Cruel School. At the camp, they enjoyed lots of evil activities, like drilling holes in one another's canoes and making fun of small woodland creatures.

And on the final day of Camp Cruel School, they headed across the lake to compete against Camp Cool School in a color war.

Let's see. . . .Who was on Camp Cruel

School's Red Team?

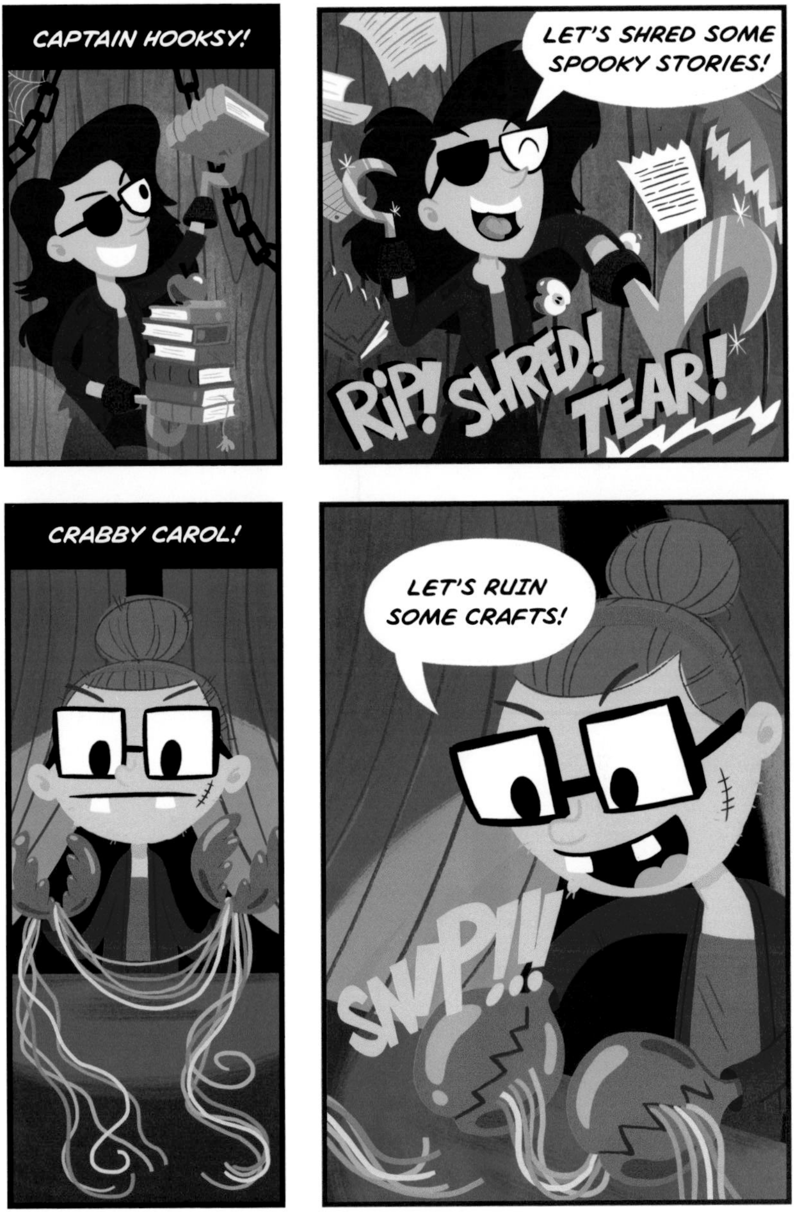
CAPTAIN HOOKSY!
LET'S SHRED SOME SPOOKY STORIES!
RIP! SHRED! TEAR!
CRABBY CAROL!
LET'S RUIN SOME CRAFTS!
SNIP!!!

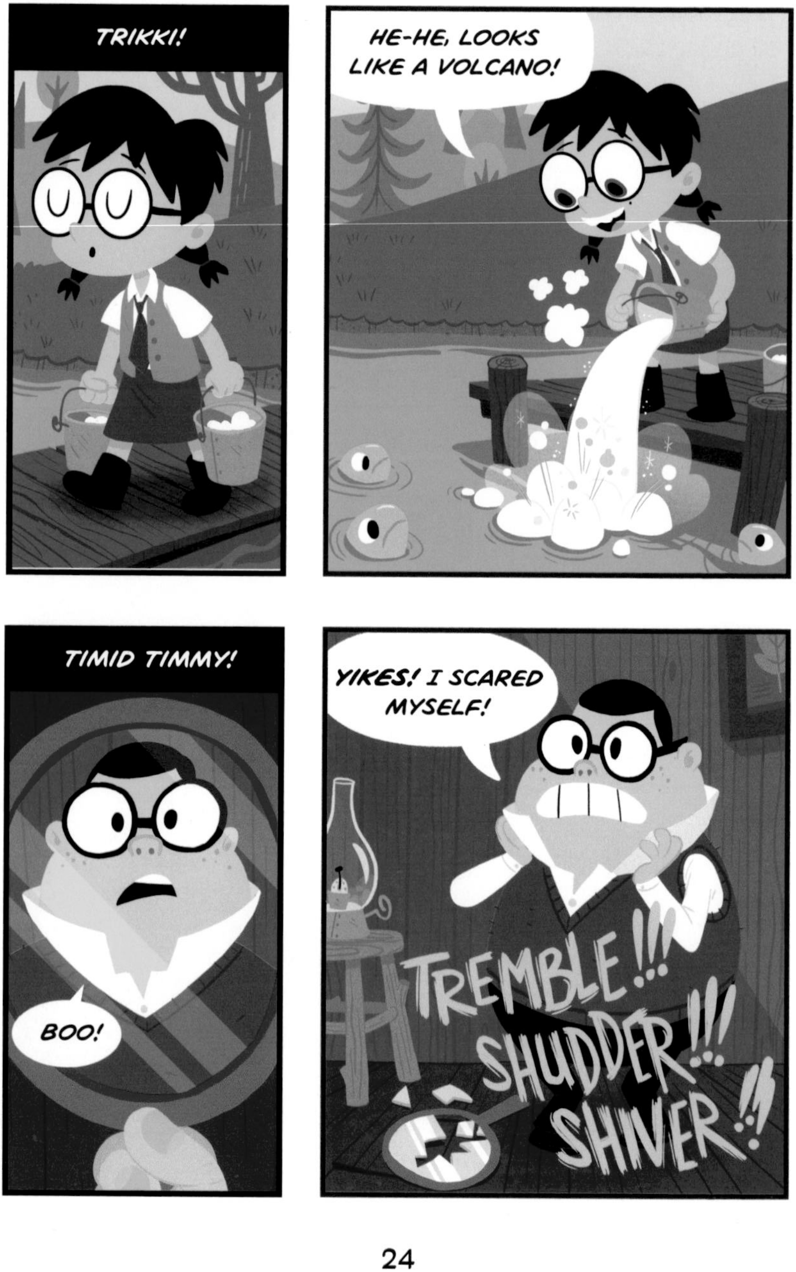
TRIKKI!
HE-HE, LOOKS LIKE A VOLCANO!
TIMID TIMMY!
BOO!
YIKES! I SCARED MYSELF!
TREMBLE!!!
SHUDDER!!!
SHIVER!!

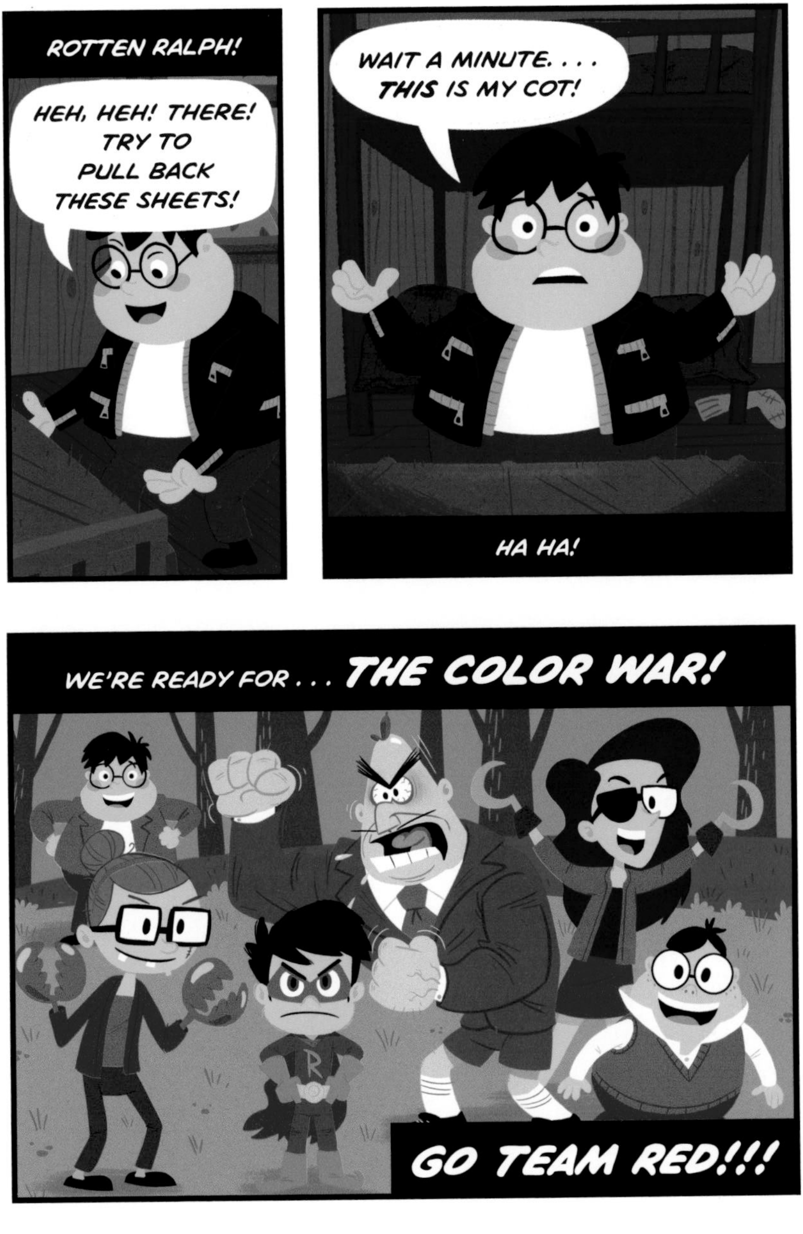
ROTTEN RALPH!
HEH, HEH! THERE! TRY TO PULL BACK THESE SHEETS!
WAIT A MINUTE. . . . THIS IS MY COT!
HA HA!
WE'RE READY FOR . . . THE COLOR WAR!
GO TEAM RED!!!

## CHAPTER THREE

**"WE'RE READY** to take you on, Team Red," Drew announced. ***"Let the color war begin!"***

"I just hope you're ready to **lose**, Team Blue!" Ray taunted.

***"No way!"*** Drew said. "Team Blue, huddle up!"

Drew wanted to give his team members a quick pep talk before the color war began. "Now I know these guys from Camp Cruel School look kind of tough . . ." he said.

**_"And creepy,"_** Ella added.

**_"And scary,"_** Crafty Carol said.

"But that doesn't mean we can't beat 'em!" Drew said. "Because we can. And we will. *Go Team Blue!*"

# "Go Team Blue!"

### cheered everyone from
### Camp Cool School.

Meanwhile, the members of the Red Team were also in a huddle. Dean Mean gave them an evil pep talk.

"Remember," he said in a low voice, "when in doubt, **_cheat!_**"

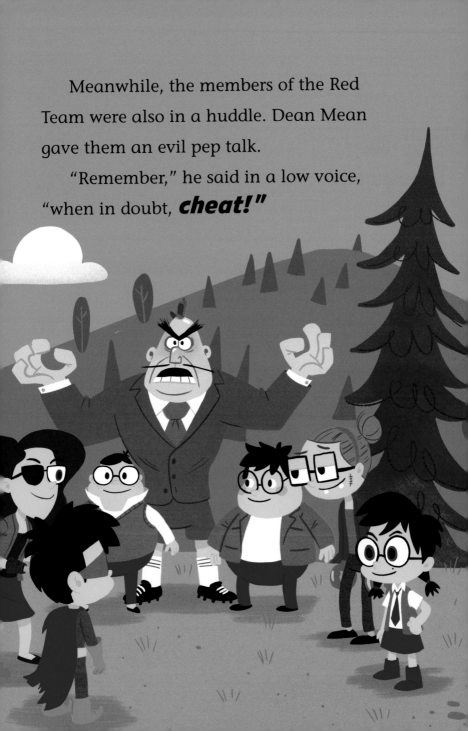

All the Cruel School campers nodded and smiled nasty smiles. Except for Timid Timmy. He looked confused. "But when you cheat, isn't that cheating?"

"Yes, Timmy, that's why it's called cheating!" Dean Mean hissed. "All the best bad guys cheat. That's how we win! Got it?"

Timmy nodded nervously. "Gee, that's not very nice. . . ."

**"Bingo!"** Dean Mean said. "Okay, Cruel Schoolers, let's get out there and cheat our way to victory. **Go Team Red!"**

"GO TEAM RED!"

roared all the Cruel School campers.

The first contest was a tug-of-war. The rules were simple. Each team grabbed one end of a rope and pulled. Whichever team pulled the other team into the stream between the two teams won.

Drew was at the front of the Blue Team
and Ray was at the front of the Red Team.
Ray tried to use his Magic Eraser to erase

**"PULL HARDER!"**
*Drew urged.*

Drew's grip on the rope, but the Blue Team gave a mighty tug, and Ray had to grab the rope with both hands.

"COME ON!"

*Ray growled.*

"My leg is itching!" Robby cried. He let go with one hand to scratch his knee, and the Red Team pulled the Blue Team closer to the stream.

"You're not beating us **that** easily," Ella insisted, pulling back as hard as she could.

"Everybody, dig in your heels in at a forty-five-degree angle!" Nikki told her teammates.

The two teams seemed to be evenly matched. Neither one could pull the other into the stream. They both strained to pull on the rope as hard as they could.

**"Bzzzz!"** A fly buzzed around in the air just behind Ms. Booksy. She was at the back of the Blue Team's line.

Simon the Frog spotted the fly. To him, it looked scrumptious. He shot out his long tongue to catch the fly . . .

**. . . *but the fly dodged it!***

Simon's long, strong tongue wrapped around the end of the tug-of-war rope.

When Simon tried to pull his tongue back into his mouth, that was just the little bit of extra power the Blue Team needed. The Red Team got pulled right into the stream.

"That's one point for Team Blue!" Drew shouted. "We won because we worked together as a team."

Everyone on the Blue Team cheered.

Everyone on the Red Team grumbled as they picked themselves up out of the stream, dripping wet.

"On the bright side," Timid Timmy suggested, "the water feels kind of good on a hot summer day." His teammates just glared at him.

Simon shot out his tongue again . . . and this time he caught the fly.

"Mmm," he said. "Victory is delicious!"

## CHAPTER FOUR

**DEAN MEAN** gathered the Red Team together. They stood far enough away from the Blue Team that the Cool School kids couldn't hear them.

"Can anyone tell me why we lost the Tug of War?" Dean Mean asked angrily.

"Because we didn't win?" guessed Timid Timmy.

**"No!"** Dean Mean roared. "We lost because we **didn't cheat** hard enough!"

Ray spoke up. "Hey, I **tried** to cheat. I tried to use my Magic Eraser!"

Dean Mean put his face right next to Ray's and growled, **"Trying** to cheat isn't **cheating**. We're bad guys! We don't **try** to cheat. We **cheat!!!"**

Timid Timmy raised his hand. "Um, Dean Mean? How do you cheat at tug-of-war? I mean, there's just a rope, and you pull on it. Whoever pulls harder wins. There's no way to cheat."

Dean Mean's face turned an even darker shade of red.

"There's **always** a way to cheat. Remember that! But forget about the tug-of-war. It's over, and we lost. But in the next game, we're going to **cheat! Got it?"**

The members of the Red Team nodded. "What is the next game, anyway?" Nikki asked.

The next battle in the color war was . . .

And how did that go for Drew Pendous and the Blue Team from Camp Cool School?

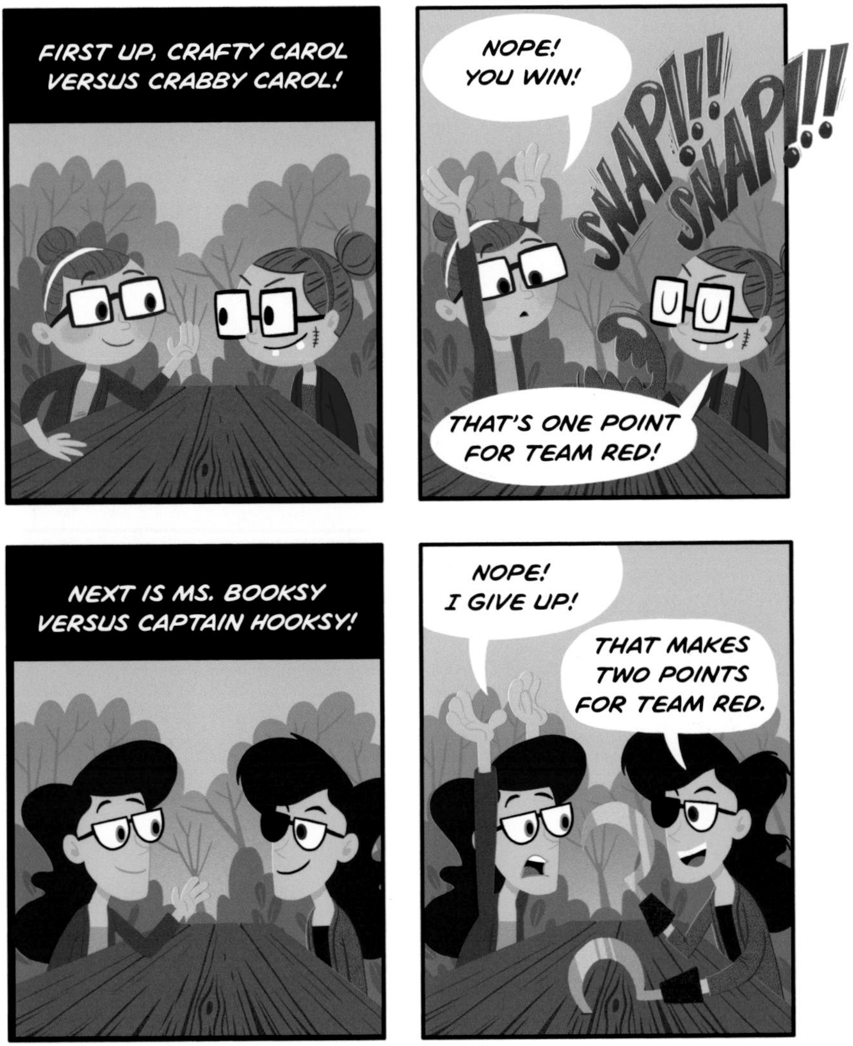
FIRST UP, CRAFTY CAROL VERSUS CRABBY CAROL!
NOPE! YOU WIN!
SNAP!!! SNAP!!!
THAT'S ONE POINT FOR TEAM RED!
NEXT IS MS. BOOKSY VERSUS CAPTAIN HOOKSY!
NOPE! I GIVE UP!
THAT MAKES TWO POINTS FOR TEAM RED.

THEN IT WAS NIKKI VERSUS TRIKKI.

HEY, NIKKI—WHAT'S THE HISTORY OF ARM WRESTLING?

INTERESTING QUESTION! ARM WRESTLING DATES BACK TO THE—

HEY, YOU TRICKED ME!

WHAM!!!

THAT MAKES THREE POINTS FOR TEAM RED!

**FINALLY,** DREW TOOK ON RAY.

YOU READY?

SURE AM!

DREW USED HIS PEN ULTIMATE TO DRAW A BIG, STRONG ARM.

ARE YOU?

OH, I'M READY.

YOUR MAGIC ERASER!

RAY USED HIS MAGIC ERASER TO ERASE DREW'S BIG ARM.

HEY!

AND THAT'S FOUR POINTS FOR TEAM RED!

43

# the BLUE TEAM

from Camp Cool School was losing, four points to one.

"I do **not** like losing," Ella told her teammates. "We've gotta work harder. Come on, guys!"

Drew patted Ella on the back. "Ella," he said. "I like your spirit. But don't worry—

we're not going to lose because there's still another contest left. And it's a big one. It's worth lots of points. Whoever wins the last contest is sure to win the color war!"

"What IS the last contest, Drew?"

Robbie asked. "Is it capture the flag? Because that would be **cool!**"

"Nope," Drew said, shaking his head. "It's not capture the flag."

"What is it?" Nikki asked.

"The last contest in the Color War is . . . **DODGEBALL!!!**" Drew shouted.

**"Yay!"** everyone cheered. They all **loved** dodgeball!

Meanwhile, Dean Mean was yelling at the Red Team.

"Why are you yelling at us?" asked Timid Timmy. "We're winning!"

"What's my name?" Dean Mean asked
Timmy.

"Um, Dean Mean . . . ?" Timmy replied.

"Yes! Dean **Mean**. I'm mean—that's
why I yell!" he screamed.

"Well, that makes sense. Got it," Timmy
said, still scared.

The two teams faced each other across
the dodgeball court. The balls started to fly,
and the players started to dodge!

CAPTAIN HOOKSY TRIED TO CHEAT BY POPPING
A BALL ON HER HOOK. BUT YOU DON'T GET ANY
POINTS FOR POPPING BALLS IN DODGEBALL.
CAPTAIN HOOKSY WAS OUT!

MS. BOOKSY DODGED THE BALL BY DISAPPEARING INTO
A STORY. BUT WHEN SHE CAME OUT OF THE STORY,
SHE GOT BOPPED BY A BALL! MS. BOOKSY WAS OUT.

Trikki pointed behind Nikki and yelled, "Look! It's the most famous scientist in the world!"

"Where?" gasped Nikki, excited. When she turned around to look, Trikki threw a ball at her!

Nikki was out.

But while Trikki was laughing about her trick, Ella **bopped** her with a ball. Trikki was out!

**BOP! BOP! BOP!** The balls flew back and forth! More and more players from both teams were out, until . . .

...*it was down to*

# DREW and RAY

They were the only two players left on the dodgeball court.

Drew got a very creative idea. Using his Pen Ultimate, he drew himself a cannon arm that could fire dodgeballs.

# "Say hello to Cannon Arm!"

### he called to Ray.

# BOOM! BOOM! BOOM!

Drew's cannon arm fired out dodgeballs, one right after the other. The dodgeballs zoomed straight toward Ray!

But as soon as the dodgeballs reached Ray, he used his Magic Eraser to erase them. "Ha! Your cannon arm's no match for my eraser, Loser Drew."

SWOOSH!!!!

Ray looked around for a ball to hurl at Drew. He spotted one on his side of the court. But as he bent down to pick it up . . .

Drew got Ray with a ball shot out of his cannon arm. ***Ray was out!***

"Yeah!" Drew cheered. "You're out. Team Blue rules, Team Red drools!"

Ray was super-mad. "Maybe I'll just erase **YOU**, Poo Pendous!" he growled, running toward Drew with his Magic Eraser.

Drew didn't like being called Poo Pendous. **"Hey!** Take that back."

"Guys!" Nikki said. "Stop fighting! I know you're archenemies and everything, but this is just a game."

"My thoughts exactly," said a familiar voice. . . .

## CHAPTER SIX

# "WHO SAID THAT?"

Rotten Ralph asked, looking around.

**"She did!"**

Ella said, pointing
up in the sky.

Everyone looked up. Hovering above
them was **Grace Cale!**

"Grace Cale!" Drew cried. "She's back!"
He'd met Grace Cale before. She was **not**
nice. She wanted to suck up all the color in
the world with her color vacuum!

What was Grace Cale doing at Camp Cool School? Well . . .

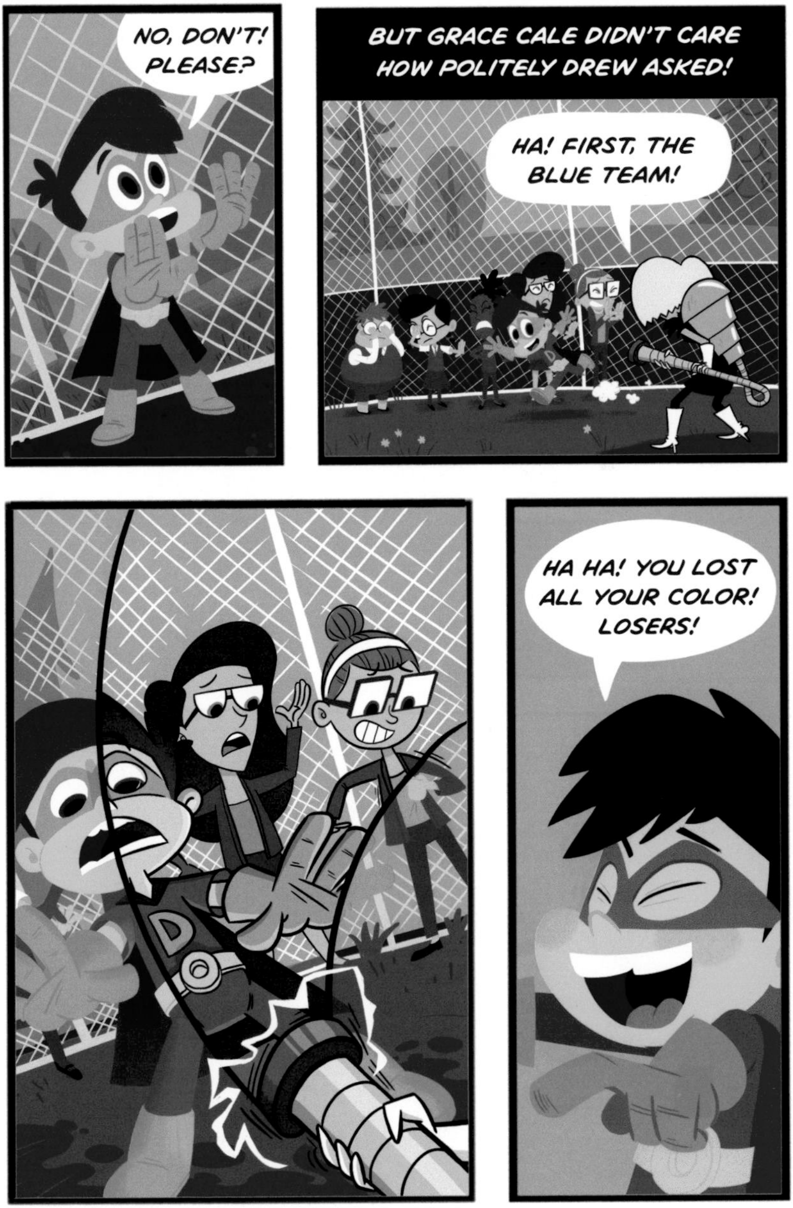
NO, DON'T! PLEASE?
BUT GRACE CALE DIDN'T CARE HOW POLITELY DREW ASKED!
HA! FIRST, THE BLUE TEAM!
HA HA! YOU LOST ALL YOUR COLOR! LOSERS!

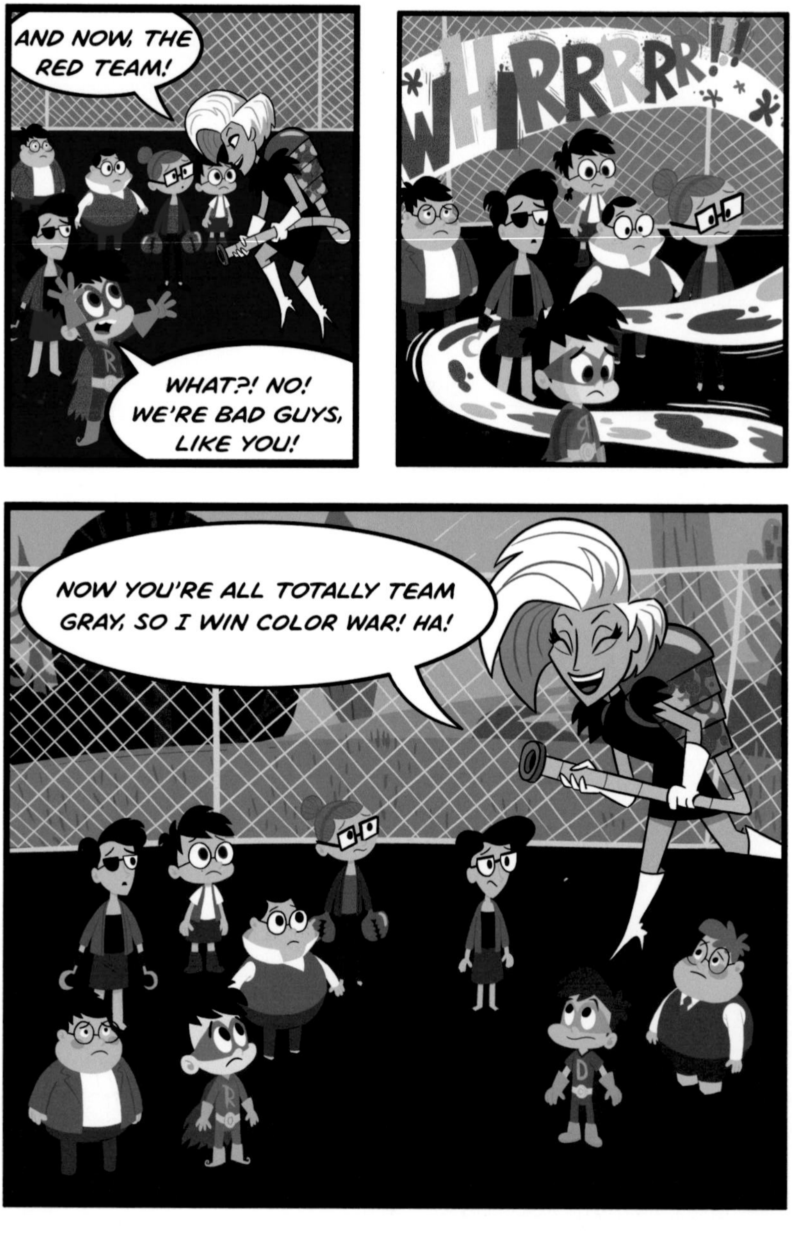
AND NOW, THE RED TEAM!
WHAT?! NO! WE'RE BAD GUYS, LIKE YOU!
WHIRRRRR!!
NOW YOU'RE ALL TOTALLY TEAM GRAY, SO I WIN COLOR WAR! HA!

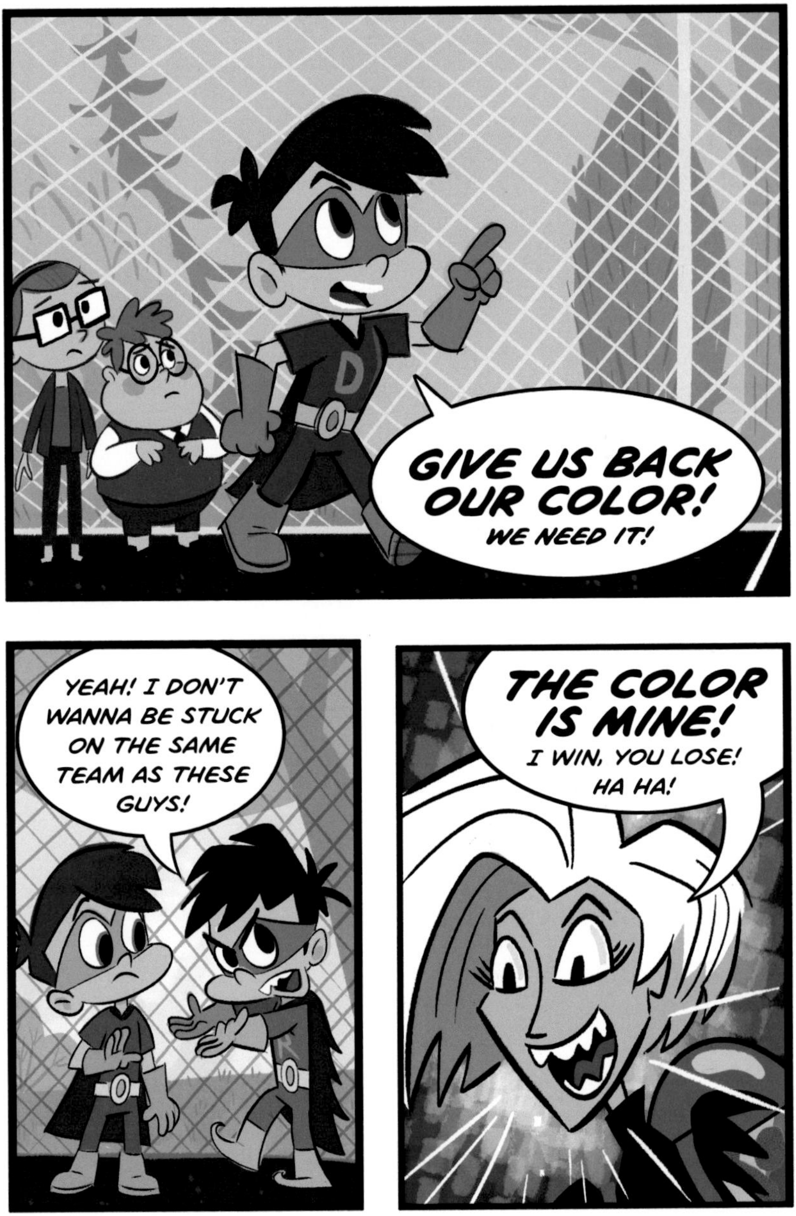
GIVE US BACK OUR COLOR!
WE NEED IT!
YEAH! I DON'T WANNA BE STUCK ON THE SAME TEAM AS THESE GUYS!
THE COLOR IS MINE!
I WIN, YOU LOSE! HA HA!

## CHAPTER SEVEN

## RAY JUMPED UP

as high as he could, trying to erase Grace with his Magic Eraser. "Give us back our color!" he yelled, "or else I'll **erase you!"**

"No way!" Grace said, laughing. She just flew a little higher into the air, out of Ray's reach.

Nikki tried to outsmart Grace. "Gee, Grace Cale, your color vacuum is so impressive! How does it work? Can I take a closer look at it?"

"So you can take your color back?" Grace sneered. **_"Forget it!"_**

Crabby Carol thought that if she could just snip the tube on Grace Cale's vacuum with her claws, all the color would fly out and they could get their color back. She climbed a tree and tried to clip the tube, but she couldn't reach it from the branch she was sitting on.

**"Hey, Grace Cale!"** Crabby Carol shouted. "I dare you to come closer to this tree!"

"Yeah?" Grace Cale said, laughing. "I dare you to come up with a less obvious

plan! You just want to snip my vacuum tube with your pincers!"

"No, I don't," Crabby Carol fibbed. "I just want to . . . um . . . oh, forget it!" She climbed back down the tree.

Ella tried to reach Grace Cale by using a trampoline. She ran, jumped on the trampoline, and bounced high into the air. *BOING*! She flew toward Grace, but the color thief saw her coming and easily flew up higher. Ella went sailing by!

***"Aaaah!"*** she yelled. She landed right in the lake.

(At least it was a hot summer day, so the cool water felt refreshing.)

Captain Hooksy thought she could use her skills as a pirate to swing on a rope and catch Grace Cale. She threw a rope around a high branch on a tree. But when she swung up, Grace Cale was just out of reach. Captain Hooksy swung back and bumped into the tree trunk.

**"Ow!"** Captain Hooksy wailed. "I mean, *ahrrrrr!*"

Crafty Carol quickly gathered up all the lanyards the Camp Cool School campers had made that summer to hold whistles and medals around their necks. She tied them together to make one extra-long lanyard. Then she tried twirling it over her head and throwing it at Grace Cale like a cowboy throwing a lasso.

But Crafty Carol wasn't a cowboy.

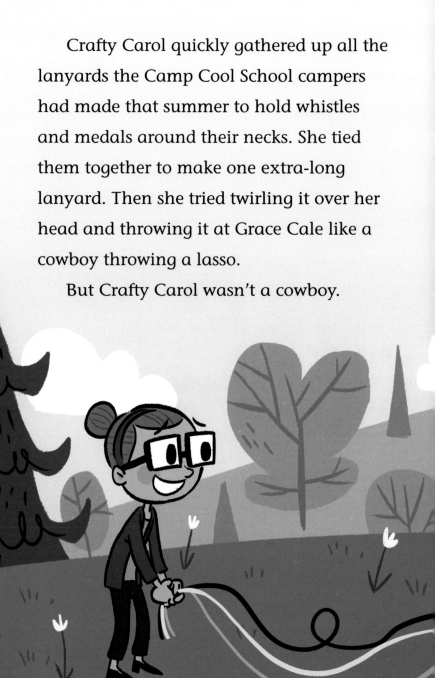

She'd never practiced throwing a lasso. She missed Grace Cale, and the long lanyard loop fell around Dean Mean.

"Whoops!" Crafty Carol said. "Sorry!"

**"Let me go!"** Dean Mean bellowed. He was really mad! Normally his face would have turned red, but Grace Cale had all the color, so his face just turned a darker shade of gray.

Drew was trying to think of something to draw with his Pen Ultimate that would get all their color back from Grace Cale. But then he thought of something else.

**"Guys!"**

he whispered to all the campers and counselors from both camps. "Come here!" He beckoned to them from the far corner of the dodgeball court.

"What is it?" Ray asked as he ran up to Drew. "We're **trying** to get our color back!!"

"I know!" Drew said. "Listen, how did
we win tug-of-war?"

"By cheating?" Dean Mean guessed.

"No—by working together as a **_team!_**"
Drew explained. "Ray, I know we're
enemies, but we both want the color back,
right?"

"Yeah," Ray said. "So what?"

"So we can work together to defeat Grace!" Drew said.

All the campers from Camp Cruel School looked confused. "Work . . . **_together?_**" Ray repeated.

"Like . . . ***as a team?***" Trikki asked.

"Yeah!" Drew, Nikki, Ella, and Robby all said at the same time.

Drew convinced the bad guys that if they joined together, they'd be more powerful as one giant team!

And so...

## CHAPTER EIGHT

### . . . THE CAMP COOL SCHOOL

campers and counselors teamed up with the Camp Cruel School campers and counselors. Together, they hatched a great plan.

"What a great plan!" Ella cheered.

**"Shh!"** Nikki said, holding her finger to her lips. "Don't let Grace Cale hear."

"What a great plan," Ella whispered.

"Okay," Drew said to all the members of Team Gray. "Does everybody understand what they're supposed to do?"

**"Yeah!"** they all said.

LET'S DO IT!

Let's see . . . What was their great plan
to get the color back?

YOO-HOO, GRACE!

WHAT DO YOU LOSERS WANT NOW?

CHECK IT OUT!

SO MUCH COLOR!

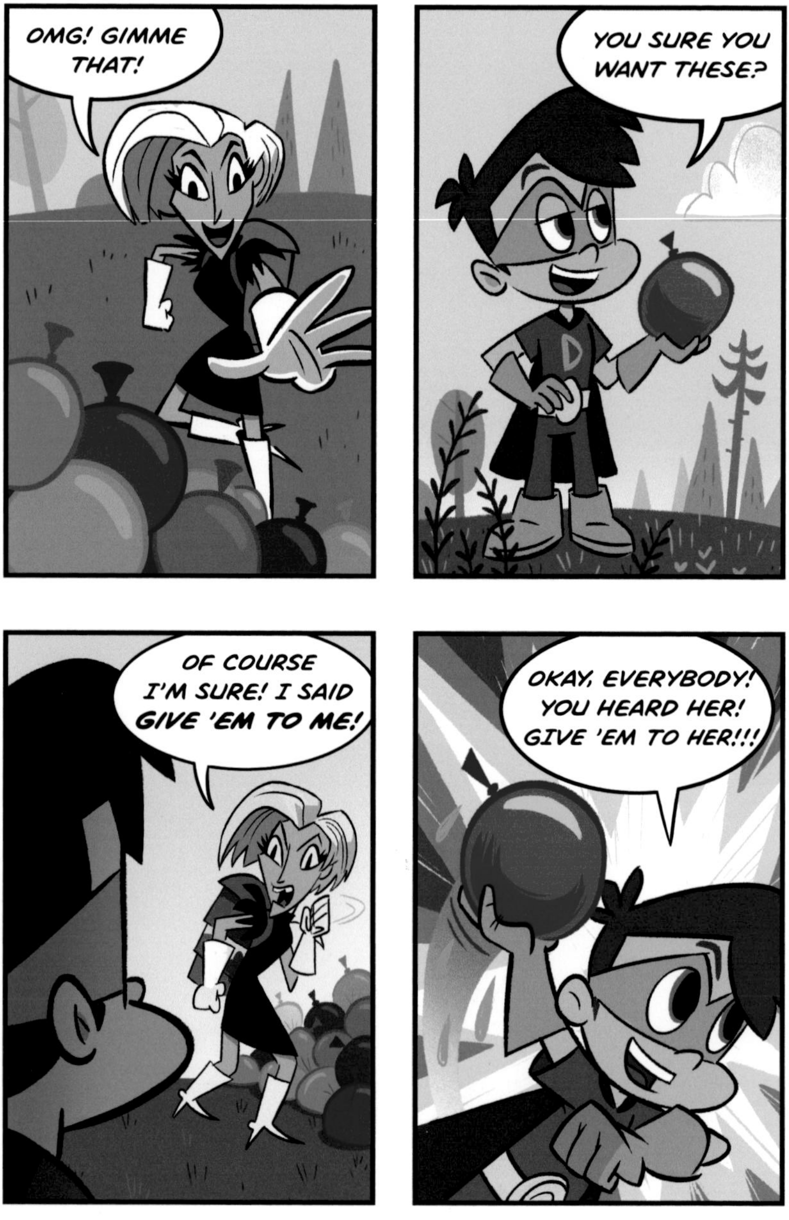
OMG! GIMME THAT!
YOU SURE YOU WANT THESE?
OF COURSE I'M SURE! I SAID GIVE 'EM TO ME!
OKAY, EVERYBODY! YOU HEARD HER! GIVE 'EM TO HER!!!

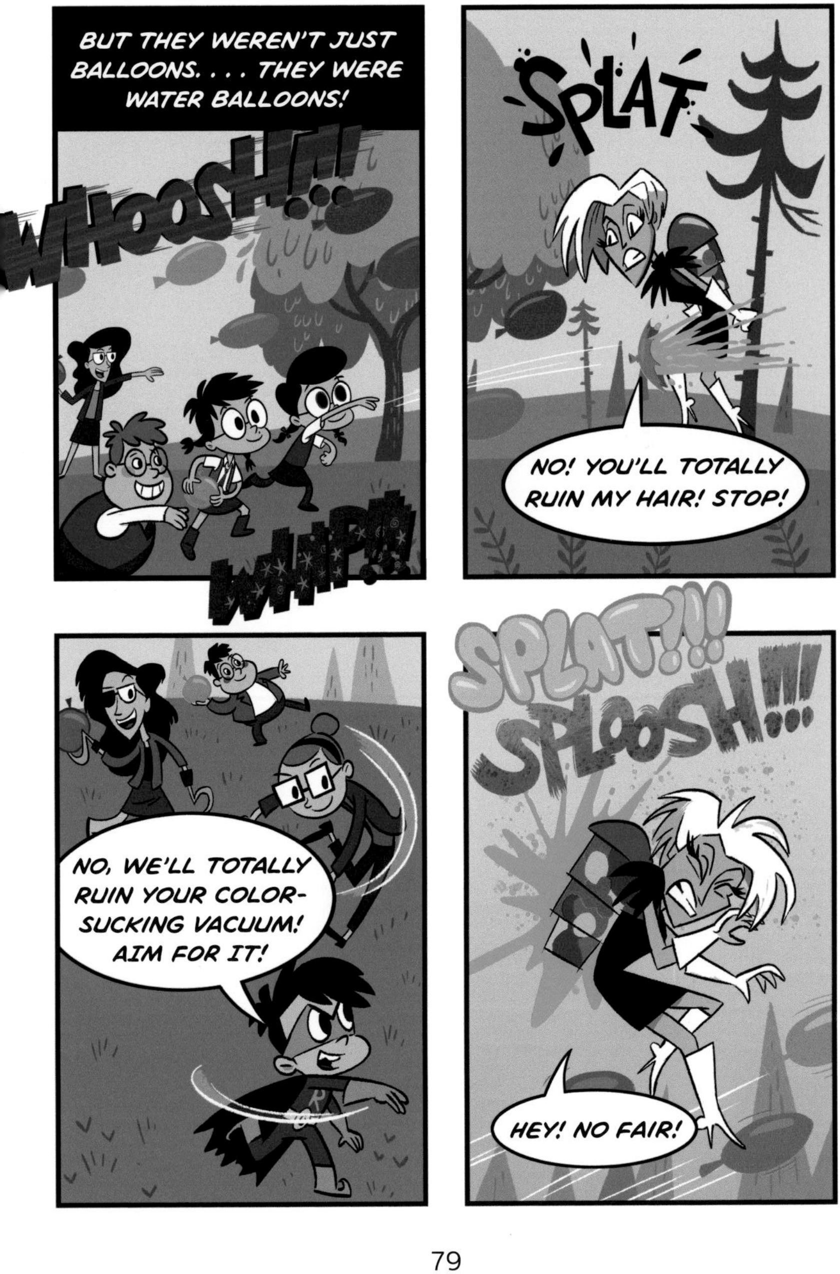
BUT THEY WEREN'T JUST BALLOONS. . . . THEY WERE WATER BALLOONS!
WHOOSH!!!
WHIP!!!
SPLAT
NO! YOU'LL TOTALLY RUIN MY HAIR! STOP!
NO, WE'LL TOTALLY RUIN YOUR COLOR-SUCKING VACUUM! AIM FOR IT!
SPLAT!!!
SPLOOSH!!!
HEY! NO FAIR!

DREW QUICKLY DREW A GIANT SLINGSHOT.

THEN HE DREW A GIANT WATER BALLOON.

HERE COMES THE MOTHER LODE!

LIKE, NOOOOOO!!!

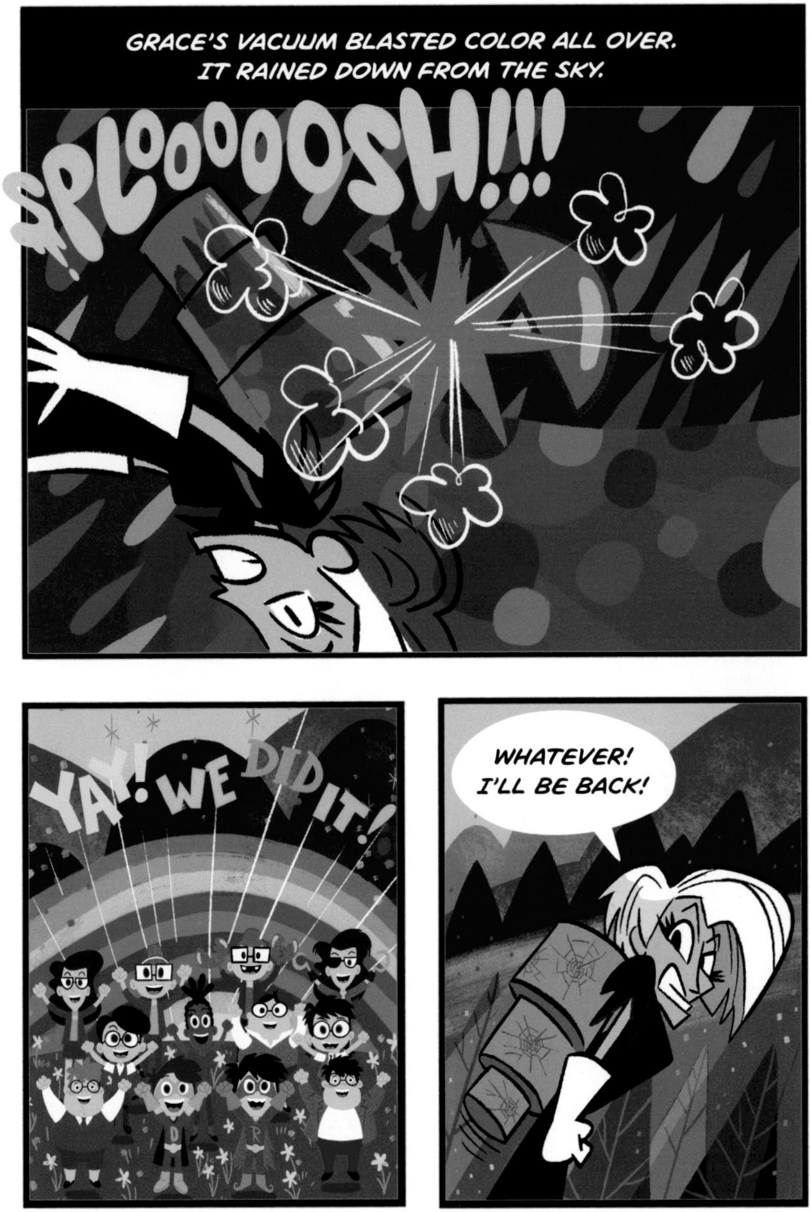
GRACE'S VACUUM BLASTED COLOR ALL OVER.
IT RAINED DOWN FROM THE SKY.
SPLOOOOOSH!!!
YAY! WE DID IT!
WHATEVER!
I'LL BE BACK!

## CHAPTER NINE

**AND THAT'S** how Ray Blank and the stupendous Drew Pendous worked together to save the camp color war! It's like they forgot they were total enemies or something!

Team Red from Camp Cruel School was dressed all in red again. ***"Yay for Team Red!"*** they cheered.

Team Blue from Camp Cool School was dressed all in blue again. ***"Yay for Team Blue!"*** they cheered.

Everything at Camp Cool School had its color back—the trees, the cabins, the lake ... **everything!** It looked much, much better than when Grace Cale had turned it all gray with her color vacuum.

"Drew," Ray said, "I gotta admit, it was a good idea to team up and work together."

"Yup," Drew agreed. "Together, the Red and Blue teams made a great team. I guess we could have been the Purple Team, except that Grace Cale stole all our color."

"Yeah," Ray said. "But if she **hadn't** stolen our color, we never would have teamed up!"

"That's true!" Drew said. "Thanks, Grace Cale! You brought us together!"

Nikki popped up right between the two enemies. "What now?" she asked.

Drew held up a water balloon. **"Well, I have an idea. . . ."**

Ray held up a water balloon, too. **"So do I. . . ."**

# WATER BALLOON FIGHT!

**they both yelled together.**
**Everyone cheered.**

Drew used his Pen Ultimate to draw lots more water balloons. As fast as he could draw them, the campers and the counselors picked them up and threw them at one another.

Everyone got soaked! But on a hot summer day, the cool water inside the balloons felt really good. Everybody laughed and squealed.

The campers didn't just throw water balloons at their own team members. They threw water balloons at campers from their **OWN** camps, too.

Crafty Carol
tossed a water balloon
at Ms. Booksy.

Captain Hooksy
popped a balloon
right over Crabby
Carol's head.

Nikki lobbed a water balloon at Robby.

**SPLOOSH!!!**

And Timid Timmy whipped a water balloon at Rotten Ralph.

**FOOMP!!!**

IT WAS THE GREATEST WATER BALLOON FIGHT EVER!!!

## CHAPTER TEN

**AT THE END** of the day, Camp Cool School was over for another summer.

"Goodbye!" Ella said to Ms. Booksy. "Thanks for all the spooky stories around the campfire!"

"Goodbye, Ella!" Ms. Booksy said. "I'll see you really soon, at Cool School."

"Goodbye!" Nikki told Crafty Carol. "Thanks for all the cool crafts."

"You're welcome," Crafty Carol said. "We'll make more crafts when you come back to Cool School!"

Drew and Robby were in their cabin, packing up. "You know what, Robby?" Drew said. "I learned something new here at Camp Cool School."

"You learned something new?" Robby asked, surprised. "Like how to make a slip knot on a water balloon?"

"I learned that teamwork is the way to go," Drew said. "Even with the Cruel Schoolers, we made a great team!"

"That's true," Robby said. "I learned something, too."

"What?" Drew asked.

"If you **triple** the crackers and chocolate and marshmallows, you can make **triple s'mores!**" Robby said, holding one up. He took a big bite.

CRUNCH!!!

Everyone was sad that camp was over.
They started to get on the bus to leave,
but then . . .

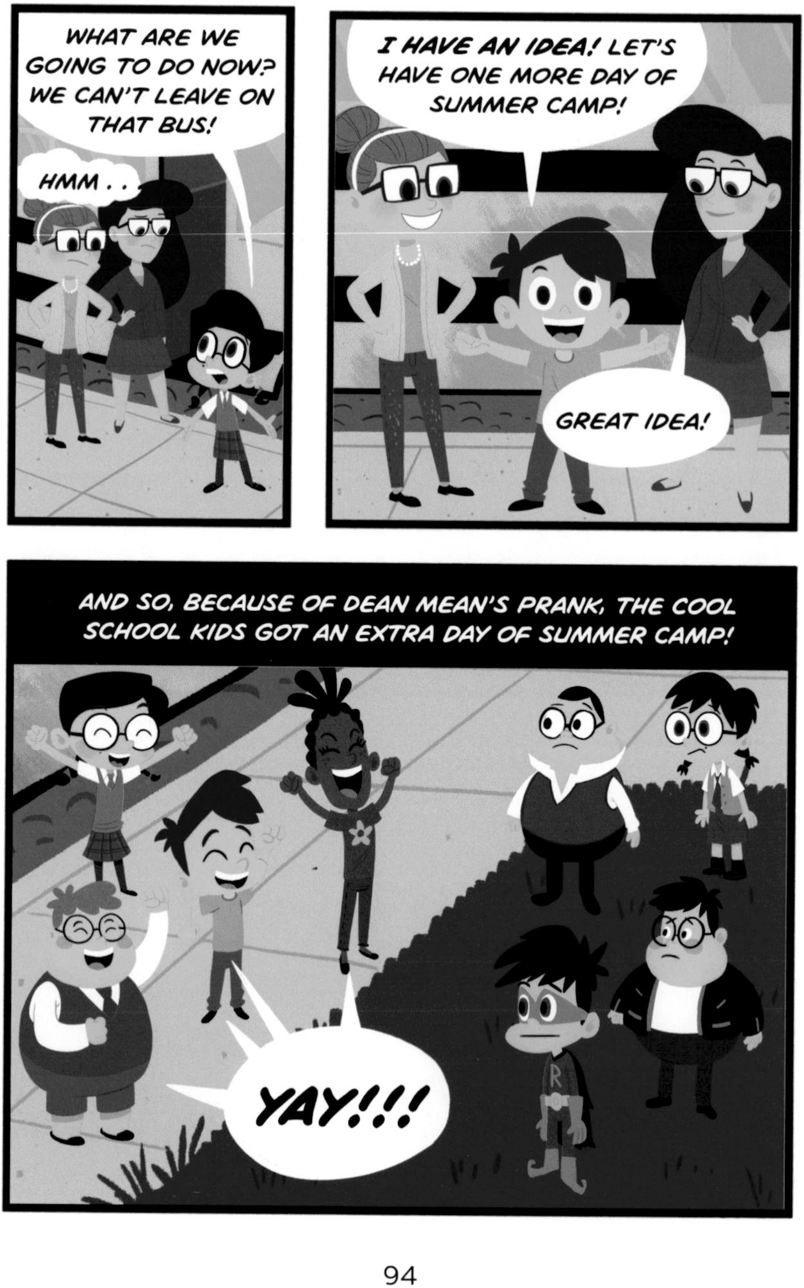
WHAT ARE WE GOING TO DO NOW? WE CAN'T LEAVE ON THAT BUS!
HMM . .
I HAVE AN IDEA! LET'S HAVE ONE MORE DAY OF SUMMER CAMP!
GREAT IDEA!
AND SO, BECAUSE OF DEAN MEAN'S PRANK, THE COOL SCHOOL KIDS GOT AN EXTRA DAY OF SUMMER CAMP!
YAY!!!!

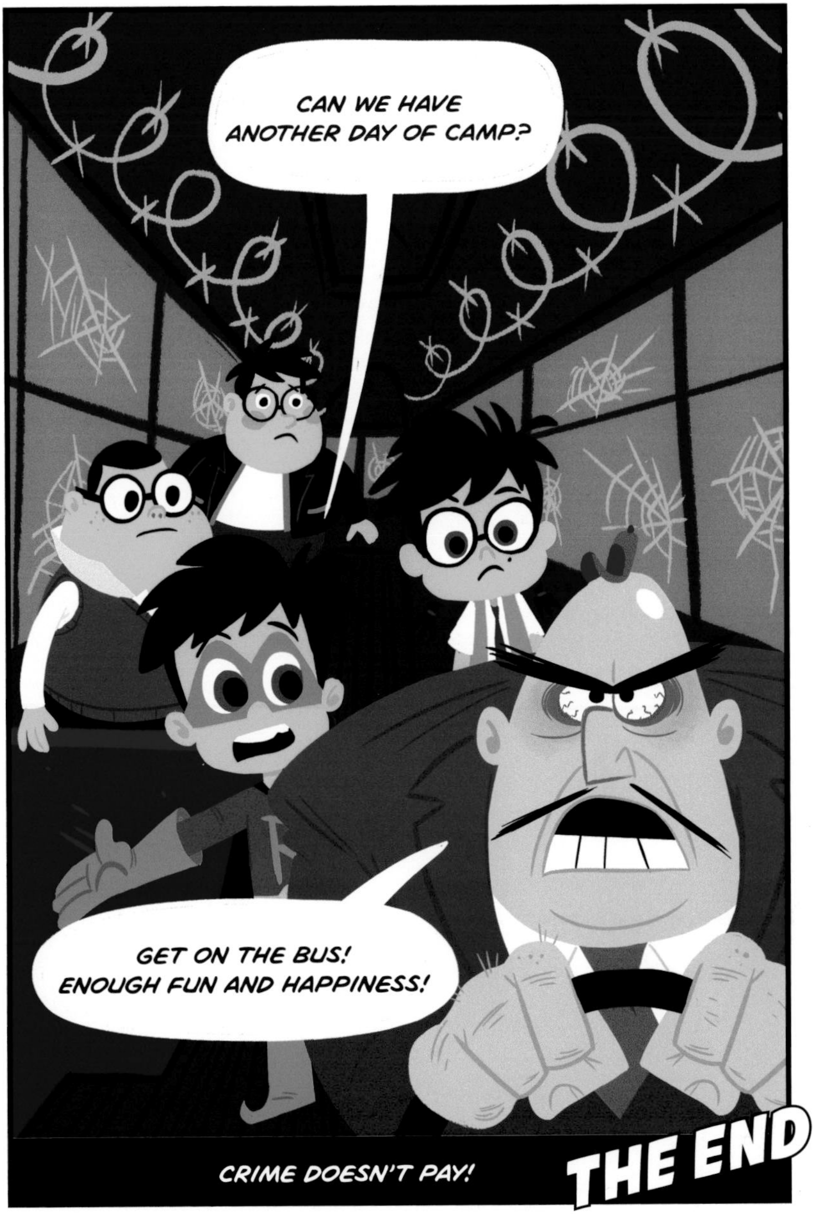
CAN WE HAVE ANOTHER DAY OF CAMP?
GET ON THE BUS! ENOUGH FUN AND HAPPINESS!
CRIME DOESN'T PAY!
THE END